Empire
of
Fairy Tales

ZsaZsa K. Louis

ARPress
ILLUMINATING IDEAS.
EMPOWERING VOICES

ARPress
45 Dan Road Suite 5
Canton MA 02021

Hotline: 1(888) 821-0229
Fax: 1(508) 545-7580

Ordering Information:
Quantity sales. Special discounts are available on quantity purchases by corporations, associations, and others. For details, contact the publisher at the address above.

Printed in the United States of America.

ISBN-13:   Softcover   979-8-89356-321-4
            eBook   979-8-89356-322-1

Library of Congress Control Number: 2024904903

Author's Note

Christmas is coming soon. I want to surprise the children with
my fairytales, that is my gift for the holidays.
I came to this country 35 years ago from a communist country Hungary,
with my son who always asked me for new fairy tales. Many years are
gone, and I enjoy my time writing books in my pension years.
I was always involved with people and I learned a lot from them as a tour
guide, as an attorney, a mental health advisor, and a poker dealer.
Many nice stories made my days better, and I hope I can provide
the same adventure for you with my fairytales.
Happy reading, and happy holidays.

People are often benefiting from daily wisdom in villages, and also from fairytales.

Nothing is new in our world; everything is repeating itself. The only new is the way we can learn about our life and about the people around us, and how we can handle ourselves. Some of these stories in my book can make us remember for others and they are refreshing our minds to see things clearly. Variety of knowledge is the spice of our life and a helpful tool to solve our problems. We enjoy listening to good stories and nice things while we travel far in our imagination because our life is not a destination; it is a journey.

I hope my fairytale book will be enjoyable for children as much as for adults.

Contents

Hannibal, The Storyteller

In the empire of fairytales are many interesting stories, characters, and animals, it would be too much to mention they all, on the same day.

A few of these were told by Hannibal who got famous for his fairytales by the children.

Hannibal was sitting on the cornerstone of the street with his old bag, in his faded clothing and waited for the children to arrive.

The children on their way to the school stopped by Hannibal every day for a new fairytale. In return one of them from the dozens, every day another gave a nice sandwich to him for his story.

Hannibal started his story and the children curiously listen:

In the Savannas lived many animals happily together. some porcupine, gophers, squirrels, rabbits, foxes, snakes, wild goats, bears, tigers, and so on.

Beautiful birds were flying from tree to tree and had sung their greetings. They waited for the rainy season for the grass to be renewed, and some trees to bring fruits.

The tiger wasn't much interested in nature's changes until he could find something to eat. He was always on a hunting expedition, therefore he always did. Goats and rabbits didn't stand a chance.

One day Mr. Tiger was taking a bath in the close creek, and it was walking toward the trees when the fire started.

Some irresponsible people made the fire to burn down the dry leaves but that was already out of hands, and the fire got the tiger's tail. The flames were close to his fur on his back but he ran back to the brook and put his tale in the water.

Luckily just on time to save his beautiful pelts, with a loud voice from his pain. That was a sad day for most of the animals who lived there because they needed to move away immediately to leave back all the hiding places and nests.

Only the tiger was happy because he could save himself and his beautiful fur.

On that day he called himself "Happy the Tiger" because he could save his life.

The Great Election

The meeting of the animals in the forest to choose their president was very important because they needed to act together to be able to survive.

Some strangers showed up; therefore, they needed to wait and postpone the voting.

Each animal got an important role, in forest life.

The birds provided the music on peaceful days, when danger was coming, they play the siren, and push the horn until everybody got in its hiding place.

The squirrels run up high on the trees to hide their nuts from the strangers.

The snakes pulled in under the bushes, and the fox was hiding behind an old tree.

The bears went into their cave with the berries in their paws, and the tiger ran away a little further to hide behind the bushes.

The goat ran with his baby in the opposite direction.

Only the owl was standing wisely on the top of the tree-like he is important, and he knew everything the best That was over very soon with the visitors, a couple of young kids who came wander around in the forest, and they were looking for berries.

When they have gone the birds had pushed the horn that the danger was over.

The animals came together on the glade of the forest to give their vote for the presidency.

The big question was who will be the best for the role?

The birds like to fly, the bears are lazy, the tiger is on hunting expedition most of his day, the squirrels are forgetful, the goat is busy with its babies, the fox can't be trusted because it is not straight forward.

It seemed that they can't come to a mutual agreement to fill the position.

That left the owl, who is the only bird which can fly without any noise, and wise too because listen first before it talks, and hide on the top of the tree where nobody can see him, but he sees everybody.

They voted all for the owl, except the snakes because they understand only signs and hiss.

The owl said thanks for the trust and continued:

"I take a 'Herculean task' for you all, therefore you all have to listen to me."

The squirrels have to hide the nuts in the same place, to be able to find it. The fox can't watch the geese, and it has to act faithfully.

The bears have to collect the dry limbs after they broke by berry picking and take it out to the side of the forest. People will not search for this side of the forest after that.

The goat has to stay with her babies close to the bushes, not walking far where I can't see them. Everybody has to pay every week one "bug" the tax for me. Anybody will break my rules, will be closed out of the forest.

The animals were thinking first but nobody aimed for the position of presidency, therefore they agreed unanimously to choose the owl.

On a dreadful day, woodworkers came to cut the trees on their side of the forest.

The birds gave the siren sound and flew away.

The president told them:

"It is an emergency, please start to move to the other side of the forest, because people are coming with heavy machinery."

They all were scared but they made it, followed the owl's advice.

Only the snakes get lost because they did not talk, they hiss. They followed the others later.

The owl said:

"We made it but don't count your chicken before they are hatched."

"You always got to be close that you are able to help one another. God save us."

There was not a better president close and far, who could give so fast such great advice.

Thanks to the owl, they all survived the change and they lived happily ever after.

The Porcupine's Couple Adventure

Mary lived on the edge of the village with his dog Pepe. The dog liked to walk in the neighboring forest and usually evening he returned.

Mary was busy with her job in the daytime and left for his dog water and food.

One evening Pepe did not return, and Mary searched for him uselessly. Mary was sad because she loved her dog and she was worried about what happened to him. She went to the animal shelter to look for him, but she did not find Pepe.

As time went by the doghouse reminded Mary of his dog every day, and she decided to give it away to the neighbors, not to be sad about it.

As she walked closer to the doghouse, she got a great surprise. She found a porcupine couple in the house. They seemed to be husband and wife.

Mary was smiling and brought them out freshwater, and a few berries.

She thought it is lucky that I still have Pepe's house. These sweet creatures needed a home anyway.

In thirty days, she got a new surprise because the porcupine couple got five children.

Now, I am a proud aunt, I better find out from the veterinarian what they like to eat. The doctor said they are like mini pigs they eat almost everything. The porcupine children did grow fast and one day the family left the doghouse. Only one of their children left behind.

Mary was wondering what happened and therefore she called the vet. The porcupine got an injury on his leg, and the doctor started to cure him.

After that he did not go away from Mary, probably he considered her his mom. He was playing with her, he rolled into a spiny ball and when Mary wanted to leave suddenly, he did straight out himself. Mary had a good time with him and looked him like earlier his dog Pepe. She gave him the name Poky.

His neighbor said:

"As we see, one door is closed, and another door is open" to make sure our life is never boring."

"I think you are lucky to have a little funny creature, like Poky."

Mary was happy but could not hug the porcupine because he rolled into a spiny ball, notwithstanding she was satisfied to have a sweet friend at her home.

Tom, the cat

The cat was beautiful, he was a tuxedo cat with a white front and paws and big green eyes.

He was walking very satisfied on the sidewalk in front of Gabriella's window. Gabriella lived alone in her condo, and her car parked in the same place every day.

Late afternoon when she arrived the cat was waiting for her at the parking lot. It was fun to see him babysitting his brothers and sisters while they were eating.

Tom acted as a bodyguard. He was sitting on a big flat stone and observed the territory with his full attention. When a dog was coming, Tom gave the sign and the cats ran under the bushes.

After several weeks of observing the cats, Gabriella came to the conclusion that the cats don't have a home and nobody care for them.

Tom was nice and friendly and he guarded his brothers and sisters all the time. He ate leftover food after his brothers and sisters.

Gabriella showed mercy for Tom and she did buy him cat food every week.

One day the people of the Animal Control Agency showed up, and started to collect the cats, also Tom's relatives.

Gabriella ran out with her old cat's carrier and invited Tom with food in. Luckily, she could save him.

It was winter already and very cold. Tom, unfortunately, got the flu. He got a high fever and he almost died. Gabriella took him to the hospital, and they could save him at the last moment before the poor cat died.

The doctor was ready to inject him and pronounce him dead, but Gabriella fought for his life. After two weeks and strong antibiotics, he got better. He was living with Gabriella in a close friendship 17 years long. He understood everything he answered every call, and he was a very clean, obedient cat.

Gabriella's love for Tom made him a perfect companion seventeen years long. She never wanted to have a cat after her earlier cat died but Tom was exceptional.

He had babysitting Gabriella when she was sick, he put his paw on her side, and he was purring.

He brought back the toy mouse to Gabriella when she threw it, and he also showed her when he hunted down a cricket. He always said goodbye when Gabriella left home. He was a perfect cat.

When Tom died, her friend said, "I am sad for your loss, because it is not easy to find a cat-like Tom was."

Gabriella kept Tom's pictures in her family album and thought about Tom for a long time.

Animals show true love and we always have to appreciate them.

The Forgotten Prince

The king palace located in the middle of the forest at the side of the river, somewhat hidden. They isolated it from the public with their own bridge, which they kept closed and private.

In front of the bridge, there was a big bullfrog, and it had sitting on a goldstone.

People wondered why is the frog in front of the entrance all the time.

It was rainy, and an exquisite carriage traveled to the palace but the bridge was closed up.

A beautiful princess did step out from her coach and turned to the frog.

I came to visit my cousin; can you help me to get in?

The frog said: "Maybe yes, maybe no, it is depending on you."

"How is that happening?" asked the beautiful princess.

The frog said:

"That is a long story but shortly if you kiss me, I can help you."

The princess went back to her carriage and turned around to leave.

Two days later she returned and ask the frog again to help her.

The frog told her the same as before and asked for her kiss.

He said:

"For your kiss, I will open the bridge and also fulfill three of your wishes.

The princess hesitated but she finally kissed the frog.

At that moment, everything changed.

The disgusting frog changed for a handsome prince, the bridge opened up, and now he did ask the princess about her wishes.

Her first question was:

"Why he turned to be a frog?"

The prince said:

"I got a hundred years of curse on me from the witch, because

I did not marry her daughter.

The second question was:

"If he could kiss her? and the prince did it Welcome.

The third question was her only wish:

"When is he going to marry her because she came to her cousin's wedding and she is younger than her?"

The prince answered I will as soon I will be sure about your love.

To prove your love, you got to find another frog at the side of the river and bring it to me.

We have to celebrate our love and freedom and show that we love everybody and everything even the frog.

They had a nice and big wedding because this prince was very rich and famous, and they invited the whole village. Everybody celebrated their love.

We may never underestimate any animal because they all have a hidden treasure.

The Famous Flute

It was a very poor shepherd boy; he was always on the look of the shepherd. He needed to take the cold in winter and the heat in summer, and he was lonely with his sheepdog at his side.

The only pleasure he got to play on his pen pipe.

He played beautifully with knowledge and passion. The people stopped on their way to listen to his music.

Even the sheep were behaving nicely when he played his songs.

He never left the sheep, and always served his time, as the owner required.

One day an old man came with a carriage and asked for his help.

He said:

"I feel bad, my heart wants to stop, I need a doctor."

"Please, take my carriage and bring here the doctor, I will watch your herd."

He believed the old man because he did not know that some bandits are waiting to steal the sheep. They took one-third of the sheep with a truck and they left with the old man.

When the shepherd boy arrived, he saw what happened. They even took his pen pipe. He was crying, and luckily the doctor witnessed his situation.

The owner didn't took him to the court, he made a complaint against the thieves.

The shepherd boy felt very unfortunate, and he was looking for another job in the city. While he was walking, he saw a second-hand shop, and his pen pipe was in the looking glass with other instruments. He went in and ask the shop owner who gave in the pen pipe?

He did buy it back from the shop.

He played a nice song to the owner and he told the name and the address of the seller. The shepherd boy went back to his owner and told him everything he knew about the deal.

Two weeks later the police found the thieves and put them in jail.

After that the shepherd boy never gave out his pen pipe, he even did sleep with it.

People are famous if they do good things, but some objects can get fame also on their own.

Kevin

The Speaking Schoolbag

Kevin hated the school, and he felt uncomfortable with the many rules and disciplines.

The only subject he found exciting history. His classmate called Kevin a New-Barbarian person to is interested only in history and bloody battles.

He knew his book inside out, and he also liked to watch many historical movies. His friend Paul was a quiet boy. He wanted mathematic, and he was very good at it.

When Kevin got a sour note from mathematic, the teacher asked Paul to help him. In return, the teacher promised him a little dog, the son of his dog.

The two students came together to study. Kevin had taught history with Paul, and Paul had taught mathematical formulas to Kevin.

The next day Kevin overslept, and suddenly he heard his schoolbag was talking:

"Wake up Kevin, today you have to write your test, remember you learned everything yesterday with Paul."

Kevin finally woke up and asked the neighbor to take him to school, not to be late.

When the test exam began, to the teacher's surprise, Kevin could answer every question.

He said: " As you can see, the will showed you the way."

"Now, I will give you an "A" because you did your best."

Also, Paul got an excellent result from history, thanks to Kevin. They were friends forever and decided to take care of the dog together when the teacher gave it to them.

The school bag was happy also because, without warning, Kevin would be late.

It is nice to be in school when we are learning and have knowledge. It is nice to be respected for doing something right. School bags are rarely talking; when they do, we got to listen to it.

Coco, the Jack

It was high noon and the agronomic Ingenieur arrived from his visit of the land with a black daw, a very smart jack.

His name was Coco. and he was very friendly.

When the family ate, he observed it from the father's shoulder.

Suddenly he changed his position when they ate cherry because he liked it very much. Very soon the bird was the favorite of the whole family.

The father let him have some cherry from the bowl while he was sitting on his shoulder. The family had placed a nice box with a flat pillow on the patio for the bird.

Coco had sleep on the patio. Occasionally, he flew over the whole neighborhood, but he always returned. It lived with the family happy for many weeks already when he suddenly disappeared. They look after Coco for two days when they found his feathers in the neighbor's garbage can close to the entrance.

They got very angry and sad because they figured their "crazy" neighbor cooked soup from Coco the jack.

They told him:

"You could ask us first when you found the bird and not kill it."

They would buy him a whole fresh chicken instead of the bird.

That was a very heartless act, but some people are not respecting birds, no matter how smart they are.

The father said, " We should keep it inside and let it out only when we were around."

Such as life, we never know what will come to make us happy or sad.

Coco was a smart bird but maybe too friendly and trusty. He didn't know danger.

Louisa, the Pig

Louisa was a very happy pig, she got everything in her life.

She had a beautiful house, a nice pool only for herself, green grass around the house and small red ball to play with.

Her owner Mimi loved her and she did everything to please her.

She got fresh cornflake with milk every morning and the cat walked out to play ball with her. She was a happy and well-shaped, clean looking pig.

The neighbors kept asking Mimi, "When will be the celebration to get some fresh pork, and bacon to eat?"

Mimi told them that would never be from Louisa. She is a house pet, not food.

One day the weather was stormy and Louisa was looking for Mimi in her kitchen because she was scared of the thunder.

She found Mimi laying on the kitchen floor and moan. The pig recognized the trouble and she ran out in the street, and she was loudly screaming.

Finally, one of the drivers was looking after the pig. Louisa turned and ran toward the house where the stranger found Mimi on the floor having a heart-attack.

He called the ambulance and luckily, they arrived fast.

They could save Mimi's life.

Louisa the faithful pig was the one who saved her owner's life and nobody wanted to believe it, when Mimi told about it later.

The neighbors did not make foolish jokes about the pork meat anymore. They realized that the biggest enemy of knowledge is the illusion of knowledge.

Lilly, the Apple-Girl

Lilly was only 11 years old. She was wearing a long red sweater and sandals.

She stood close to the newspaper stand with her big basket and sold apples every day. Her mom was sick, and she could not work. Lilly needed to make the extra money because they got only a low amount of unemployment support from the government.

Lilly took her job very seriously, and she went on the street every day after school to sell apples. Some of her friends called her apple-Lilly and bullied her.

She did not care because she was worried about her mother a lot. It was already winter, and she still stood on the street in her sweater but she felt cold.

One of the women felt sorrow to see her shiver and offered her coat. Lilly sai thank you much and rejected it.

Her nose and her hands were already blue from the cold.

Suddenly, out of nowhere, an older man showed up and he said:

"I cannot bear to see you suffer; I want to buy your whole basket of apple just tell me the price."

Lilly was hesitating and said fifty dollars.

The gentleman pulled out a hundred-dollar bill and he gave it to Lilly.

She was very happy and said thank you three times, notwithstanding her feet already were hurting from the cold. She was running home happy to tell her mom about the man.

She entered the door and yelled:

"Mom, I sold it all! We can buy a coat now."

She got no answer, she found her mom laying in her bed dead. She did not know what to do.

She ran over to the neighbor Aunt Amy, and she was crying non-stop.

They were shocked by the news and took Lilly in. They arranged everything and called up Lilly's relatives in the neighboring city.

There are days in our life when we could fly from happiness but in reality, from bad news, our soul can click out in a minute. Lilly felt that she is going to die after her mom also. Lilly grew up and still visited the neighbors who took care of her in her pain and sorrow.

The Clown

Allen was a child with special needs, and he did only six years of elementary school. He went to work for the circus when he was 16 years old. His parents were happy that he liked the circus and helped him to do things right. Allen was busy with the horses. He fed and cleaned them. It seemed that he is satisfied with his job.

One day he was the helper to lead the horse on the stage and he saw the clowns are acting with one another. He found it very funny.

After this day when he finished his work, he went close to the stage and watched the clowns. He liked their colorful clothing and their round red nose.

One of the clowns was more friendly with him and asked if he wants to try it. He borrowed his red ball shape nose and run on the stage while the other clown rolled in a small ball. He did not see it and step on it.

He had a big fall, and he was told. "You have just learned your first trick; we all have to learn sometimes."

He got pain in his left arm for a couple of days, but he did not give up learning to be a clown.

He brought with him his bike to show them some tricks. He was very good at it. The circus owner told him to change his cloth and put up the nose, the next day he can be in the show.

The circus was full, everybody wanted to see the clown with the bike. Allen was looking funny and nice in his clown outfit, and his parent wanted to see him also.

Everything was going alright but in the last round, his bike ran out of him. Luckily, he did not fall, he made only a friendly somersault for the public.

The people liked him and they all yelled once more, so he did it, and he was happy to have success.

His parent also did buy him a new bike, just in case. Allen was very happy and loved his new bike. He did practice on it all the time.

He kept saying:

"Practice makes perfect..."

Happiness lives in us in our daily life, we just have to find it.

Mary's Cockatoo

Mary was a widow, and she lived in the garden city of Virginia with his bird Leon the cockatoo. Leon was glossy black with a red tail. She always was busy to say something to Mary, when the bird had to see her.

Mary felt lonely, therefore she started to teach Leon to talk. First, they practiced the numbers.

Leon said: "One, two, three, come with me".

Mary was laughing about the bird funny talk.

After that, they said their names and asked, "How are you, Leon, and you Mary?"

Leon learned easily and fast.

When he said nicely the words Mary had feed him with grass seed. They were happy and cozy together.

Complications started only when Mary's boyfriend Joe showed up. He was seemingly jealous of the bird, and he acted foolishly with Leon, saying bad words. Like: shut up, get the hell out, and so on.

The bird repeated back what he said.

One day he visited Mary drunk, and they argued.

Mary said:

"Get out Joe. I cannot stand you; you are like an animal."

Joe left and slammed the door. The bird got scared and said.

"Leon doesn't like it."

Mary said I do not like it either. Joe is crazy when he drinks.

Next time we will tell him: "Get out crazy Joe."

That was going on for a while and Leon got better and better with his speech.

Joe showed up and the bird was quiet for a short time, but Mary got upset with Joe to drinking too much again, and said:

"Get out Joe and please, do not come back"

Then suddenly the bird said:" Get out crazy, I do not like you, get the hell."

Mary needed to laugh at how adequate Leon told off Joe.

Mary and Leon lived happily ever after, Mary thought, it is better to be the partner of a cockatoo, then a drunkard tottering boyfriend.

Ralph, the Church Mouse

Ralph was a teeny-weeny white mouse, who lived in the church under the Altair, in a small town. He was very comfortable there, he shared his place only with a small spider. It was in the other corner of the Altair. It was only one thing that bothered him, the food supply.

It was coming rarely, and not in his favor. Without cheese and bacon, he did not like his day. He tried to please himself to run over to the restaurant across the street, but even at night was dangerous for him, because some kind of car always run by. Of course, they did not push the horn because they could not see him.

One day while he was on his hunting expedition, he found a nice warm coat, on the ramp of the walkway and it was also a half-sandwich in its pocket.

What a great dinner, said Ralph to himself. "Just like in my dream! Here is a cheeseburger!"

Ralph was overly happy, he ate, and he had fallen asleep. The next morning, he woke up in the suburb at the side of a garbage can. The coat had belonged to a homeless man, who positioned himself to the arcade of an old storage building. Ralph was sad that his nice home in the church was not available and started to look for new food in the garbage can. He found there only an old apple and dry bread. He didn't want to get entangled in any suspicious business, therefore he waited for his next ride.

He decided to go back to the church. He was thinking and thinking.

Which road is the shortest one to go home? Suddenly a truck showed up and threw out the garbage in the dumpster. Ralph ran up in the truck and was hopeful to get to the church.

For his misfortune, the truck drove outside of the town, and Ralph was crying. In this way, I never going to get home.

How can I go home? It is too far for me to walk, and also scary.

They arrived at the gasoline station and Ralph did look for another car. He found a new red car with a young lady, who seemed to be nice. Ralph ran over in her car and he arrived back in the town.

He fell asleep and when he woke up the girl held him in her hand and talked to him

Are you going to be my mouse, I feed you and take care of you. Okay, my baby?

Ralph was very happy and did stay with the girl. The girl was also happy because she was lonesome.

While they ate breakfast, Ralph was also sitting on the chair and was singing a silly little song:

"Welcome here for me, good by the church".

I can be religious without church too.

It is nice to have love and a good home, even a mouse is happy about Ralph and the girl lived happily ever after, and both of them favored cheeseburger.

The Witchdoctor

It was a small village behind the hills, where only two farmer's families and a few other families lived. Most of them worked and helped on the farms.

One sunny day in summer a man arrived with a one-horse carriage and moved in, in the old tobacco store building. He was in his fifties, with a friendly stomach, and a nice smile. His name was Tony, and he was a witchdoctor.

Officially, we could call him a doctor helper. He could detect health problems and write recipes and he also knew few natural remedies.

In more serious cases he needed to call the ambulance, and occasionally, he played the role of a veterinarian also.

He put his important equipment on the shelves behind him: like Epsom salt, alcohol, Bengay, some bandages, different herbal teas, like chamomile tea, peppermint tea, green tea. They all got great remedies. The chamomile tea alone can reduce stomachache, muscle spasms, inflammation boosts immunity, good against insomnia, and reduces stress.

He was right to advertise it to the people in his village to buy it. Tony was ready to serve. He also kept his cellular phone plugged in, to be ready for the good or bad news.

He was not a charlatan like "witchdoctors" in Africa, who had hit the patient's head with fist on a drumbeat, until they lose consciousness.

No, he was far from these methods. He told uncle Hugo to go to the riverside to fish with a bottle of chamomile tea, against his headaches, because he knew that Aunt Julia gave him the stress. His medication worked well. After a few days of separation aunt, Julia took the lunch for him to the riverside, where they got the peace.

When aunt Greta twisted her ankle, he told her to go home with her cane slowly and soak her leg in Epsom salt, after that put over some Bangey place it on the pillow. She can read fairytales for her grandchildren in the next 3-4 days.

One of his patient Rudy brought his cat on Friday the 13th to him and said:

"This poor cat is sick; he doesn't want to eat."

He examined the cat's stomach and told him your cat ate something heavy, like stone, or maybe something else. Rudy said, I just remember, my seal-ring disappeared from my nightstand. Probably, he played with it and snacked it down.

Tony said:

"I can tell you two good news, your cat will survive, but need a cut, and it also seems to me that Friday the 13th is your lucky day. You can take the cat to the veterinarian's hospital and they will cure him.

He did practice his witch until on the weekend he got called to a funeral, and when he did look at the dead person his hand dropped at his side.

It was a sixty-year-old man, and he routinely examined him in his coffin. He realized that the man is still in life. He put in his mouth a little Jagermeister what he always got in his pocket, and the man had suddenly seat up. At first, the people got shocked only for a short time.

The whole village started to celebrate him and called him the doctor of the year. The man's name was Franc and he gave him a new carriage for appreciation.

It was only one case; he could not solve.

Uncle Andrew walked with his geese and Tony asked how is he doing.

He said:

"I am fine, but my geese are perishing."

Tony said:

"You should walk with them to the river where the grass is not poisoned

with the smog of the cars".

Two weeks later they met, and Tony asked about the geese.

Uncle Andrew said:

"They are still not better".

The doctor said give them to drink some chamomile tea, that will help.

A month later they met again, and Tony asked about the geese.

Uncle Andrew said:

"They all perished."

Tony answered:

"I am sad because I would have a few more good advice"

After that, some people started to joke and said:

"Don't give me your advice because that can make perish the geese."

LET'S COLOR!